ナ7672)

★ SPORTS STARS ★

PETE SAMPRAS
STROKES OF GENIUS

BY MARK STEWART

Children's Press®
A Division of Grolier Publishing
New York London Hong Kong Sydney
Danbury, Connecticut

Photo Credits
Photographs ©: Allsport USA: 46 (Mike Hewitt), 34 bottom (Clive Mason), 27 (Mike Powell), 39, 45 right (Gary M. Prior), 25, 44 left (Rick Stewart); AP/Wide World Photos: 34 top (Charles Bennett), 43 (Mark Lennihan), 15 (Rene Macura), 37, 45 left (Michael Probst), 40 (Dave Thomson); Corbis-Bettmann: 29 (S. Carmona), 31, 44 right (Ales Fevzer); John Klein: cover; Palos Verdes Peninsula High School, Triton Yearbook, 1986: 10, 17; Russ Adams: 18, 22; SportsChrome East/West: 6 (Andreas Rentz/Bongarts Photography), 47 (H. Schneider/Bongarts Photography), 3 (Rob Tringali Jr.).

Visit Children's Press® on the Internet at:
http://publishing.grolier.com

Library of Congress Cataloging-in-Publication Data

Stewart, Mark.
   Pete Sampras : strokes of genius / by Mark Stewart.
     p. cm. — (Sports stars)
     Summary: A biography of the professional tennis player, discussing his childhood, Grand Slam championships, personal tragedies, goals, and behavior on the court.
     ISBN 0-516-22049-7 (lib. bdg.)   0-516-27074-5 (pbk.)
     1. Sampras, Pete—Juvenile literature. 2. Tennis players—United States—Biography—Juvenile literature. [1. Sampras, Pete. 2. Tennis players.] I. Title. II. Series.
GV994.S16 S74 2000
796.342'092—dc21
                                                00-026712

© 2000 by Children's Press®, a Division of Grolier Publishing Co., Inc.
All rights reserved. Published simultaneously in Canada.
Printed in the United States of America.
1 2 3 4 5 6 7 8 9 10 R 09 08 07 06 05 04 03 02 01 00

CONTENTS

CHAPTER 1
The Shot Maker 7

CHAPTER 2
Having a Ball 9

CHAPTER 3
Prescription for Progress 14

CHAPTER 4
Pete Who? 21

CHAPTER 5
Wanting It 26

CHAPTER 6
Sad Farewell 32

CHAPTER 7
Gunning for Greatness 36

Chronology 44

Statistics 47

About the Author 48

THE SHOT MAKER

Pete Sampras is in a jam. His opponent has driven him back behind the baseline with a wicked serve, and only a perfect backhand lob has kept him in the point. As the two players exchange ground strokes, Pete uses everything in his bag of tricks to move his man to the left side of the court. Suddenly, he unleashes a booming forehand to the right corner.

Now it is Pete's opponent who is in trouble. His eyes widen and his nostrils flare as he scampers desperately to save the point. A lunging backhand floats high across the net and Pete charges in to meet it. As he takes to the air, the ball is more than a dozen feet off the ground—well out of reach for most players on the men's tennis tour.

Pete coils in midair then snaps forward at the top of his jump. His racket smashes the ball, blasting it past his bewildered opponent at more than 100 miles per hour (mph). For a six-footer who can dunk a basketball, this one was easy.

Thousands of fans roar their approval. Thousands more simply shake their heads. Is there *any* shot Pete can't make? On this day, at least, the answer is no. It is another straight-set wipeout for the man who has dominated his sport for a decade, and shows no signs of letting up.

HAVING A BALL

Thwock! Thwock! Thwock! When Sam and Georgia Sampras first heard this strange noise echoing through the house, they thought something had gone wrong with the furnace. Luckily, it was just Pete, their little boy. He had found an old wooden tennis racket, and was joyfully smacking a ball against the basement wall. Thwock! Thwock! Thwock! The racket felt good in Pete's hand and the swing came naturally. "I enjoyed the feel of the ball on my racket," he remembers.

Pete and Stella are the tennis-playing stars of the Sampras family. Stella went on to become a college tennis coach.

The Samprases had four children—Gus, Stella, Pete, and Marion. When Pete was seven, his parents decided to move the family to California. They strapped all their possessions onto the roof of their station wagon and drove across country to Rancho Palos Verdes, near Los Angeles.

After they settled in, Sam took Pete and his older sister, Stella, to the tennis courts near their home. He watched in amazement as Pete chased down every shot and whacked the ball with great speed and accuracy. The boy had never set foot on a tennis court before, yet he looked as if he had been playing his entire life.

Convinced that Pete was a natural, Sam took his son to the nearby Jack Kramer Tennis Club and began looking for a coach. Sam hoped that Pete would catch the eye of a top teaching pro. Instead, a man named Pete Fischer caught *Sam's* eye. A pediatrician with a genius-level IQ, Fischer was a lousy player who had never actually coached anyone in his life. But Fischer seemed to have some very good ideas when it came to teaching kids, so Sam asked what he would charge to instruct Pete. Fischer liked the idea of being a coach. He said he would teach the seven-year-old for free.

Dr. Fischer was astounded by Pete's natural ability. The only thing the boy lacked was an understanding of how the game was actually played. This, of course, was the good doctor's specialty. "He's a very weird guy," says Pete of his first coach, "but brilliant. He couldn't play tennis, but he knew how it should be played. He tried to put his brain in my body."

Much of Pete's training took place off the court. He and Fischer would watch films of great players and discuss what made them great. Fischer pumped Pete's mind full of the history of the game, and talked about the importance of the four "Grand Slam" tournaments—the United States Open, French Open, Australian Open, and Wimbledon. Often, the doctor had dinner with the Samprases. "He seemed like part of the family," Pete recalls.

Slowly but surely, Pete developed into an excellent player. His forehand was flawless, and his backhand was strong. As he grew, his serve became extremely powerful. And as his serve got better, he was able to improve his volleying skills. By the age of 10, Pete already knew what he wanted to be—a professional tennis star.

★ ★ ★

Being a great young player had its drawbacks, though. Pete did not have many friends, and his parents were too nervous to watch him play. They would drop him off at tournaments and then show up after the finals to drive him home. "Here I was," Pete remembers, "playing against older kids, and I felt alone. Maybe that's where I got my independence and the way I am on the court. I was just out there by myself."

★ 3 ★

PRESCRIPTION FOR PROGRESS

Pete rose steadily in the junior rankings from 1980 to 1984. Always playing older boys, always trying new things, and almost always winning—he was one of the world's top players for his age. Dr. Fischer, however, believed Pete needed to change his game to keep improving. He told Pete that he had to abandon his two-handed backhand and switch to a one-handed grip. He would be able to reach more balls, explained his coach, and he would be able to do more things with the ball.

To convince Pete, Fischer pointed to Rod Laver, who had become Pete's favorite player.

Pete and Andre Agassi flank Rod Laver, whom many consider the greatest all-around player in tennis history.

The Australian star of the 1960s and 1970s could hit every shot in the book and win on any type of surface. Fischer told Pete that Laver used a one-handed backhand with excellent results. He could smash winners down the line, loft gentle lobs, or drive opponents crazy with slices, spins, and chop shots. Hoping to equal Laver's 11 Grand Slam singles titles, Pete was persuaded to try the one-hander.

The first time Pete hit a one-handed backhand, the ball flew over the fence. The timing was entirely different, and the ball was much harder to control. When Pete's opponents realized that he had abandoned his two-handed backhand, they zeroed in for the kill. They pounded balls to Pete's left and then waited for him to hit into the net or out of the court. Players he had once demolished with ease were now destroying him.

Pete's ranking plummeted. The other kids were telling him to get rid of Fischer. Pete did not know what to do, but in the end, he had no

Pete (kneeling, center) may be the smallest kid in the picture, but at 14 he was already the best player on his high school team.

choice. He trusted his coach. "To have everyone picking on my backhand was very frustrating," Pete says of the year he spent perfecting his new shot. "But eventually everything started coming together. Switching to the one-hander turned out to be the best thing I could have done for my tennis."

By this time, Pete had grown to be six feet tall, and he could hit his serve with breathtaking force. In 1987, he was selected to play against the

Pete explodes into a forehand at the 1989 U.S. Open. He won 18 matches in 1989 to reach number 81 in the world rankings.

top teenagers in the world as a member of the United States Junior Davis Cup team. He also beat top-seeded Michael Chang at the U.S. Open Junior Championships.

When he was 16, Pete was ready to turn professional. He knew what he wanted to do with his life, and he felt he was ready. Dr. Fischer assured Pete and his parents that this was the right decision. At 110 to 120 mph, Pete's serve was his major weapon. His backhand was good enough to keep opponents at bay, while his forehand was powerful enough to hit for clean winners. He joined the Association of Tennis Professionals (ATP) Tour in 1988, played in 10 events, and won half of his matches. When the season ended, he was ranked in the Top 100.

In 1989, Pete won 18 of 37 singles matches to reach number 81 in the world rankings. His best moment came at the Italian Open, when he and

★ ★ ★

Jim Courier—a friend from his days as a junior—won the doubles championship. Toward the end of the 1989 season, Pete made a big decision. It was now time to break away from Dr. Fischer. There was nothing more Fischer could teach him.

4

PETE WHO?

Early in the 1990 season, Pete defeated Andres Gomez to win his first tournament—the Pro Indoor Singles Championship in Philadelphia. Four months later he won a tour event in Manchester, England. These victories led many to believe he was ready to ambush the game's top stars the following week at Wimbledon, but he lost in the very first round.

After this disappointment, Pete set his sights on the U.S. Open. He played well the rest of the summer and rose to number 12 in the rankings. After solid wins in the first four rounds of the U.S. Open, Pete had to play Ivan Lendl, the top-ranked player on the tour. Ten months

Pete bends low for a volley during the 1990 U.S. Open. His victory at the age of 19 shocked the tennis world.

★ ★ ★

earlier, Lendl had invited Pete to his home to help prepare Lendl for the Masters tournament in Madison Square Garden. In return, Lendl gave Pete a taste of what it was like to be the world's best player. Pete was amazed at how hard Lendl worked to stay at the top. He trained for many hours a day, slept 12 hours a night, and put nothing into his body that did not benefit his tennis game. Pete took those lessons to heart.

Now, less than a year later, Pete earned a chance to unseat his mentor. Their match was a titanic struggle. In the final set, Pete's serving and play at the net were flawless, and he won 6–2 to advance to the semifinals.

In the semifinals, Pete faced John McEnroe. Although McEnroe battled valiantly and had Pete at his mercy a couple of times, he simply could not overcome the 19-year-old's awesome power. Pete won in four sets to earn a spot in the U.S. Open final against an old rival from the juniors—Andre Agassi.

★ ★ ★

In the hours prior to their match, Pete devised a strategy he was sure would work. Tennis is a game of angles—Dr. Fischer had constantly drilled this into Pete's head. By coming to the net, you reduce your opponent's angles. In their final, Pete sprinted to the net against Agassi whenever he had the chance. No matter how hard Agassi hit the ball against Pete that day, Pete was able to volley the shots right back for winners. He won easily, becoming the youngest champion in U.S. Open history.

Pete hoists the 1990 U.S. Open trophy and listens to the crowd's roar. He would soon discover that defending a title can be harder than winning it.

WANTING IT

Pete soon learned the hard lesson every young champion learns—getting to the top is a lot easier than staying there. As one of the game's bright young stars, Pete played in tournaments and exhibitions almost every week. This left him little chance to practice and try new things—and almost no time to rest between events. To make matters worse, the shoes Pete had agreed to endorse were giving him shin splints! "I didn't know what I was doing, and my game wasn't really ready," he says of the years following his remarkable victory at the 1990 U.S. Open. "I was kind of thrown to the wolves."

Pete looks skyward after winning the 1992 Davis Cup. Teammates Andre Agassi, Jim Courier, and John McEnroe are on the left and captain Tom Gorman is on the right.

Although Pete maintained a high ranking and was a member of America's champion Davis Cup team in 1992, he did not win another Grand Slam tournament for almost three years. The low point during this time came at the 1992 U.S. Open. Pete reached the final, where he faced Stefan Edberg. Whenever Edberg needed a big shot, he seemed to get it. When Pete needed one, however, he did not always come through. The Swedish star triumphed in four sets. "I lost the match and it really bothered me for months," Pete says. "It ate at me. I didn't want it enough. It changed my career."

★ ★ ★

After the loss to Edberg, Pete began to accept what his new coach, Tim Gullikson, had been trying to tell him since coming aboard earlier that season. Gullikson had a deep understanding of tennis, and knew what it took to win a match. Ramming a serve down someone's throat or bashing a forehand out of his reach did not make you a complete player, he kept telling Pete. A true champion knows how to "build" points a shot at a time. He had to learn how to move a player around the court, get him just where he wanted him, and then make a strong shot or hit a volley to end the point. By the following summer, Pete was a changed man.

Pete's first big victory in 1993 came at Wimbledon. The tournament's slick grass surface favored his powerful game. Pete's serve now streaked across the net at more than 120 mph. When receiving serve, he now knew how to hang in points until he had an opportunity to win them. On July 4, Pete defeated his friend Jim Courier in a thrilling "all-American" final.

Pete accepts Jim Courier's congratulations after winning Wimbledon in 1993. It was his first Grand Slam title in nearly three years.

★ ★ ★

After the final, Pete acted as if a great weight had been lifted from his shoulders. He was relaxed and joyful. He even joked with the press.

By the end of that summer, Pete was on a roll. At the U.S. Open, he sliced through the draw like a surgeon. He lost his serve just seven times in seven matches. In the final, Pete broke Cedric Pioline's serve to begin each set. Rarely had a U.S. Open champ dominated his competition so completely.

Pete won the next Grand Slam tournament—the 1994 Australian Open. In the final, he beat Todd Martin, whose coach was Tom Gullikson—the twin brother of Pete's coach. He continued to play fantastic tennis throughout the year, winning a total of 10 events, including his second Wimbledon. Like his idol, Rod Laver, Pete won championships on every surface in 1994—grass, clay, carpet, and hard court. Pete was on track to have one of the greatest seasons in tennis history when foot and hamstring injuries ruined the second half of the year. His first half had been so good, however, that he was still the top-ranked player when the season ended.

Pete signs autographs for British fans in 1994.

SAD FAREWELL

What should have been Pete's most joyful year turned out to be a season of sorrow. During the 1995 Australian Open, Tim Gullikson collapsed. X rays revealed the awful truth—there were four tumors on Gullikson's brain. He was dying of cancer. Gullikson flew back to Chicago during the tournament, leaving Pete all by himself. Suddenly, tennis just did not seem so important.

Pete did not want to let down the fans, so he tried to play his quarterfinal match against Jim Courier. Pete cleared his head and played well for four sets, but as the fifth set began he could no longer block out the sadness. "It hit me like a ton of bricks," he remembers. "I sat down at a changeover at the start of the fifth and all of a sudden I had this vision in my head of Tim lying in the hospital bed. I just couldn't get it out of my head."

Pete began to weep. He could not stop. He tried to play through the tears, but found it impossible. No one knew what to do. The tension was incredible. Thousands of people were watching the world's best player having a breakdown, and millions more witnessed it on television. Pete was about to give up when his old friend came to the rescue. From across the net, Courier shouted, "We can do this tomorrow!"

The wisecrack woke Pete up. He composed himself and won the match. To this day, Pete sees it as kind of a milestone in his career. "It was good to get it out," he says. "I just released every emotion I had at the time. It's ironic it happened in front of a lot of people. I never show emotion."

Less than a year earlier, another friend of Pete's—former Top 10 star Vitas Gerulaitis—had died in a freak accident. These tragedies, coming

A somber Pete acts as a pallbearer at coach Tim Gullikson's funeral.

The crowd goes wild as Pete celebrates his third Wimbledon championship in a row.

so close together, confused Pete. Everything had gone so well for him in his life that he was not sure how to handle it. Pete credits his father with helping him through this tough time with a lot of love and a large dose of reality. "He just looked at me and said, 'Pete, you've lived in this perfect world of yours for a long time. Real life's not like that. This is part of real life.'"

Pete began thinking very seriously about life. He decided that the best way to honor his friends was to try to become what they believed he could be—the greatest tennis player in history. He started in England, winning his third straight Wimbledon.

Then, at the 1995 U.S. Open, he met Andre Agassi in the final, just as he had five years earlier. Agassi held the number-one ranking, and Pete wanted it back. Pete dominated three of the four sets played that day to win his third U.S. Open. By the end of the year he was number one again.

GUNNING FOR GREATNESS

Over the next three years, Pete took great strides toward his goal of becoming the greatest. Challengers came and went, but no one had the staying power to pull ahead of Pete in the rankings for more than a few weeks at a time. In 1996, he won the U.S. Open again. In 1997, he won his second Australian Open and fourth Wimbledon, and held the top spot in the rankings every single week.

In 1998, Pete won Wimbledon again, and finished the year as the ATP Tour's number-one player for the sixth time in a row. No one had ever done that before. Understandably, it is the accomplishment Pete cherishes the most.

When it comes to finishing first, Pete takes the cake. In 1998, he was the ATP Tour's number-one player for the sixth year in a row.

Pete finally slipped from the top of the rankings in 1999, though hardly because of the competition. A nagging leg injury slowed him during the season's first few months, causing him to miss several important events. When he was healthy, however, Pete beat everyone in sight. He won his sixth Wimbledon that summer to tie Roy Emerson for the career record of 12 Grand Slam singles titles, then returned to the United States to win events in Los Angeles and Cincinnati.

For a moment, it looked as if Pete would catch Andre Agassi—who was having a terrific year—and get back his number-one ranking. But the day before the U.S. Open, Pete injured his back in practice and had to pull out. More than two months passed before he was able to play again. By the season-ending ATP Tour Championships, Agassi had locked up the top spot. But it was not too late for Pete to make a point. He rolled to the final and destroyed Andre in straight sets.

Pete makes it 12 Grand Slam singles titles with a victory at Wimbledon in 1999. He finished the year tied with Roy Emerson for the career record.

Pete poses with America's top-ranked woman player, Lindsay Davenport, at the 1999 Wimbledon Champions Ball.

⭐ ⭐ ⭐

As long as Pete plays, he will stay focused on his goals. He wants to establish a record for Grand Slam titles that will be impossible to match. He also wants to win the French Open—the one slam that has eluded him. And he refuses to settle for being anything less than the top-ranked player in his sport. "You need the game, you need the heart, you need the mind," he says about being number one. "Some guys have a little bit of everything, some guys have two out of three. But in order to do it for six years, you need all of them. You have to want to be number one. And I want it more than anyone."

As Pete works on the final chapters of his tennis career, he wants to enrich his life in other ways. He wants to spend more time with his parents, he wants to get better at his next sport—golf—and he wants to raise more money for the six charities he supports. "Everyone needs help at times, and everyone has the ability to help," he says. "It means a lot to me to have a positive impact on people's lives."

★ ★ ★

How would Pete like to be remembered when all is said and done? Though he may never admit it, Pete hopes fans will think of him as the best ever. There have been times when he has felt humbled by tennis, but there have also been times when he has felt complete mastery over the game.

All Pete Sampras really wants is to receive the recognition he has earned. That may sound like a strange thing to say about someone who has broken almost every record there is, but sometimes Pete makes winning look so easy that many fans have no idea how hard he works—or even how good he is. "It's flattering in some weird way," he says. "But at times," he admits, "you want people to appreciate how difficult it is."

Though some fans do not appreciate how hard Pete plays, they never fail to let him know how much they adore him.

C ★ H ★ R ★ O ★ N

1971	• August 12: Pete is born in Washington, D.C.
1978	• Pete begins taking lessons from Dr. Peter Fischer.
1987	• Pete defeats top-ranked junior, Michael Chang.
1988	• Pete turns pro and joins ATP Tour.
1989	• Pete wins the Italian Open doubles with Jim Courier.
1990	• Pete becomes the youngest winner of the U.S. Open.
1992	• Pete becomes a member of the champion Davis Cup team.

O ★ L ★ O ★ G ★ Y

1993	• Pete wins Wimbledon and the U.S. Open.
1994	• Pete wins the Australian Open and Wimbledon.
1995	• Pete earns his third career Wimbledon and U.S. Open titles.
1996	• Pete wins the U.S. Open again.
1997	• Pete wins the Australian Open and his fourth Wimbledon; he is voted the top player in ATP Tour history.
1998	• Pete wins Wimbledon for the fifth time.
1999	• Pete wins his sixth Wimbledon. He is the youngest athlete on ESPN's All-Time Top 50 list.

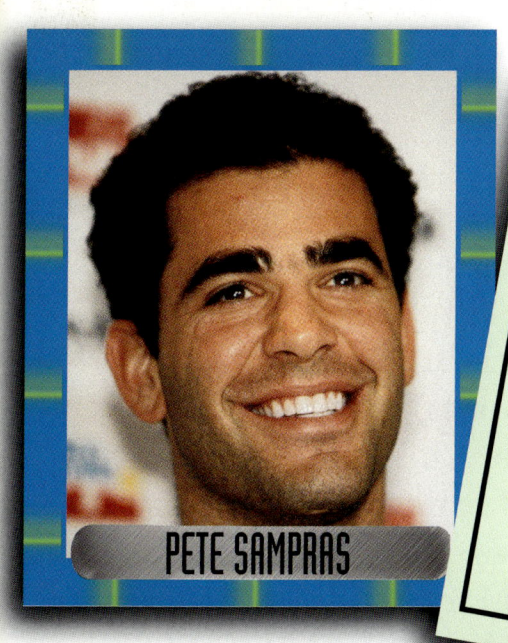

HONORS AND CHAMPIONSHIPS

U.S. Open Singles Champion	**1990, 1993, 1995, 1996**
Wimbledon Singles Champion	**1993–1995 & 1997–1999**
Australian Open Singles Champion	**1994 & 1997**
Davis Cup Champion	**1992 & 1995**
ATP Player of the Year	**1993–1998**
USOC Sportsman of the Year	**1997**

ABOUT THE AUTHOR

Mark Stewart has written hundreds of features and more than fifty books about sports for young readers. A nationally syndicated columnist ("Mark My Words"), he lives and works in New Jersey. For Children's Press, Stewart is the author of more than twenty books in the Sports Stars series, including biographies of Monica Seles, Pedro Martinez, Drew Bledsoe, and Mia Hamm. He is also the author of the Watts History of Sports, a six-volume history of auto racing, baseball, basketball, football, hockey, and soccer.